Where do eggs come from?

Elen Rhys

Illustrations
Michael Price

Gomer

'I'm in the mood for cooking!' sang Ogi as he did a little dance.

   'But what shall I cook?' he muttered. 'Mmmm? Oh, I know! BOBIPANCAKES!'

   So he looked in his bobirecipe book.

'Right! I need flour, eggs and milk,' said Ogi.

'Where is the flour?' he asked.

'We don't have any flour left,' said Nib.

'Where are the eggs?' asked Ogi.

'I ate the last one for breakfast,' said Bobin.

'Where is the milk then?' he asked.

'I poured the last drop on my cereal,' answered Nib.

Ogi shook his head. 'But how can I make bobipancakes without flour, milk and eggs?'

'Right!' said Ogi suddenly. 'There's only one thing to do.'
'What?' answered Nib and Bobin.
'You'll have to go to the shop to buy me some flour, milk and eggs.'
'But we can't,' said Nib.
'No,' agreed Bobin. 'The shop is closed in Abernog today.'

'Oh dear!' sighed Ogi. 'Where do flour, eggs and milk come from before they go to the shop then?'

Nib, Bobin and Ogi weren't sure of the answer.

'Maybe they grow on trees,' said Nib

'Or maybe they grow in the garden,' suggested Bobin.

'Or maybe . . .' started Ogi before his thoughts were interrupted by a hooting noise outside.

It was Ffion the Farmer.

'Hello you three!' shouted Ffion. Nogdog barked.

'And hello to you too, Nogdog!' she laughed.

'Would you like to come with me to my farm?'

'Oh, yes please,' smiled Nib and Bobin.

'How about you Ogi, do you want to come too?'

'Well, I was going to cook some bobipancakes, but I don't have the ingredients.'

'I might be able to help you there,' winked Ffion. 'Hop on!'

'We're the bob, bob, bobinogs!' sang the three on their way to Ffion's farm. Nogdog barked the tune too. They had never been to a farm before and they were very excited.

'Wow! This farm is bobintastic,' said Ogi.
'Oh, you haven't seen anything yet,' replied Ffion.
'But Nogdog has!' laughed Bobin. 'Look!'
Nogdog had found a little friend.
'Follow me, we've got lots to see,' said Ffion.

'This is where I grow golden wheat,' explained Ffion.
'Wheat? Why do you grow wheat?' asked Ogi.
'To make flour of course,' smiled Ffion.

'Oh! I know what that is!' said Nib. 'A cow.'

'Yes, Bobiblod the cow. But do you know why I keep her on my farm?' asked Ffion.

'I do!' said Bobin.

She walked up to Bobiblod and pulled her tail.

'Moooooooooo!' mooed Bobiblod angrily.

SPLAT!

Bobin jumped in fright and nearly got covered from head to toe in warm brown muck.

Everyone laughed. Ffion sat on a special stool.
'Look carefully!' said Ffion.
She held Bobiblod's udders and milked her.
'Milk!' said the three Bobinogs in surprise.
'Yes,' smiled Ffion, 'all lovely, warm and fresh.'

Next, Ffion the Farmer took the Bobinogs to the hen-house.
Nib hid behind Bobin.
'Scaredy-cat,' giggled Ogi.
'No, scaredy-hen!' giggled Bobin.

'Don't worry, Nib!' said Ffion. 'My hens are very friendly and very useful too.'

'Why?' whispered Nib.

Suddenly a hen gave a big cluck and laid . . .

'An egg!' said the three Bobinogs in surprise.

'Yes,' smiled Ffion.

'Now come with me to the house, I have a surprise for you Ogi,' winked Ffion.

Ffion put some flour, milk and eggs on the table.
    'There,' said Ffion. 'The ingredients you need to make some bobipancakes, Ogi.'

'*I'm in the mood for cooking!*' sang Ogi as he did a little dance.

In a blink of a bobinogs eye, Ogi had cooked some delicious bobipancakes.

'Mmmm. These are bobitastic,' said Nib as she gobbled her third bobipancake.

Everyone agreed, including Nogdog.

'Thanks Ogi,' said Ffion.

'Thank you,' said Ogi. 'We've had a wonderful time on the farm so now we've got a surprise for you too.'

The Bobinogs sang Ffion a special song to say a special thank you for a special day.

'Flour comes from golden wheat
And milk comes from the cow
Eggs come from the clucking hens
Let's make some pancakes now!
Come and sing along with us
Bobbily, bobbily, boo, boo, boo
The farm is really so much fun
Bobibye, bye bye, toodle doo.'